JoJo &
Winnie
AGAIN

MORE Sister Stories

JoJo & Winnie: Sister Stories

Surprise Party

Another Day

Ghosts in the Family

Thirteen Going on Seven

What My Sister Remembered

Circles

At the Sound of the Beep

Just Like a Friend

Matt's Mitt & Fleet-Footed Florence

Fran Ellen's House

Almost Fifteen

Baby Sister

Underdog

Thunderbird

The Fat Girl

Fourteen

Beach Towels

Call Me Ruth

Bus Ride

Class Pictures

Hello. . . . Wrong Number

A Summer's Lease

A Secret Friend

A December Tale

Dorrie's Book

A Pocket Full of Seeds

The Truth About Mary Rose

The Bears' House

Marv

Peter and Veronica

Veronica Ganz

Amy and Laura

Laura's Luck

Amy Moves In

JoJo & Winnie AGAIN

MORE Sister Stories

by **Marilyn Sachs**

illustrated by MEREDITH JOHNSON

Dutton Children's Books

New York

Copyright © 2000 by Marilyn Sachs
Illustrations copyright © 2000 by Meredith Johnson

Library of Congress Cataloging-in-Publication Data
Sachs, Marilyn.
JoJo & Winnie again: more sister stories / by Marilyn Sachs; illustrated by Meredith Johnson.—1st ed. p. cm

Summary: More adventures of JoJo and her younger sister Winnie.
ISBN 0-525-46393-3 (hc)
[1. Sisters—Fiction.] I. Title: JoJo and Winnie again.
II. Johnson, Meredith, ill. III Title.
PZ7.S1187 Jq 2000   [Fic]—dc21   00-026215

Published in the United States by Dutton Children's Books,
a division of Penguin Putnam Books for Young Readers
345 Hudson Street, New York, New York 10014
www.penguinputnam.com
Designed by Alan Carr • First Edition
Printed in USA
1   3   5   7   9   10   8   6   4   2

With love to Sam—
fourth grandchild and
first grandson
—M.S.

For Andi and Nicole
—M.J.

Contents

JoJo & Winnie

AGAIN

MORE Sister Stories

Chapter 1

The Wrong Doll

When JoJo was nearly ten, she loved looking through the catalog of *Dolls from Faraway Lands*. Each page showed a doll from a different country. The Japanese doll wore a purple silk kimono with delicate green and white designs. The Dutch doll had a white lace cap and wooden shoes. All of the dolls were beautiful.

"Which one do you like best?" her sister, Winnie, kept asking her. Winnie was six.

"I can't decide," said JoJo. "What about you?"

3

"I like this one," said Winnie, pointing to the doll from France. "I like her blue beret and her white boots and tight skirt."

Just before Christmas, JoJo decided which doll was her favorite. "This one," she told Winnie. "The doll from China. I love her long, shiny black hair. And look at how her red satin pajamas are decorated with all those tiny, gold dragons!"

She told Mom, and she told Dad. "I wish I had this doll. I want her more than anything else in the whole world." She winked at her parents. "I hope Santa Claus brings her for me."

So—to nobody's surprise—JoJo got the Chinese doll for Christmas. And Winnie got the French doll.

"She's even prettier than in the picture," JoJo cried, lifting the beautiful doll out of her box. "Oh, thank you, Mom! Thank you, Daddy!" She hurried over to kiss each of them. "And thank you, Santa Claus," she added quickly when Mom motioned with her head in Winnie's direction.

Winnie pulled her doll out of its box and burst into tears.

"What is it, Winnie? What's wrong?" asked Mom.

"It's the wrong doll," Winnie sobbed. "I hate her."

"But you've been telling us the doll from France was the one you liked best."

"Not anymore," Winnie howled. "I hate her."

"Calm down," Dad said. "You have to make up your mind and not keep changing it."

"I'm not going to change it," Winnie bawled. "I hate this doll, and I'll always hate her!" She slammed the doll back into its box.

"Be careful," Mom said wearily. "I guess if you really don't like the doll, we can send her back and exchange her for one you do like. I think I know where Santa got her. But you'll have to be

sure this time that you're not going to change your mind."

"I'm sure," Winnie said. "And I'll never, never change my mind."

"All right, then," Mom said. "Which doll do you want?"

Winnie looked over at JoJo cradling her doll. "That one," she said.

After a lot of screams and insults, JoJo and Winnie were sent up to their separate rooms for a time-out. A time-out lasted the same number of minutes as each girl's age—six minutes for Winnie, nine and a half for JoJo. Downstairs, Mom and Dad sounded as if they needed a time-out, too. Each girl, after slamming her door, opened it again to listen.

"Why not?" Dad insisted. "Why shouldn't she have any doll she likes? What difference does it make?"

"It makes a difference to JoJo. Winnie can have any other doll except the Chinese doll."

"JoJo is just being selfish, and you're taking her part," Dad yelled.

"And you always take Winnie's part!" shouted Mom.

"No, I don't!"

"Yes, you do!"

The girls glared at each other from behind the partially opened doors of their rooms.

"You're such a brat," JoJo said. "You're always copying me."

"No, I'm not."

"Yes, you are."

Each girl went back into her room and slammed the door.

After a few seconds, JoJo opened her door. Winnie opened hers.

"If you get the Chinese doll, I'll never let you come into my room again."

Winnie shrugged.

"And I'll never let you play with my puzzles."

"Who cares? They're too hard anyway."

"And I'll never, never talk to you as long as I live."

Each girl went back into her room and slammed the door again.

After a few seconds, JoJo opened her door again. Winnie opened hers.

"Are you really going to exchange your doll for the Chinese doll?"

"Yes."

"Are you absolutely sure you are?"

"I'm sure."

"Absolutely, positively sure?"

"Yes."

"Good, because I've decided to change my mind, too. You can have my Chinese doll, and I'll take your French doll. She is adorable in her little blue beret, her white boots, and tight skirt."

"No!" Winnie yelled.

"Why not?" JoJo demanded.

"Because . . . because . . . I don't want you to have my French doll."

"But it *won't* be yours; it will be mine. And you'll have the Chinese doll. Isn't that what you want?"

"No. It's not fair!" Winnie shouted. But Mom and Dad were yelling so loud at each other downstairs that they couldn't hear.

"I have another idea," JoJo said sweetly. "We could each keep our own dolls and have fun together. They could visit each other and maybe try on each other's clothes."

Winnie didn't say anything.

"They could have slumber parties sometimes," JoJo continued.

Winnie still didn't say anything.

"And I could take pictures of them together, having tea with my little blue and white china tea set. I'll even put the pictures in my photo album."

JoJo took wonderful photographs and put the special ones into a beautiful album. Everyone admired her photos. There were very few pictures of Winnie in JoJo's album.

Winnie took a deep breath. JoJo watched and waited.

"Will I be in the pictures, too?" Winnie wanted to know.

"I guess so," JoJo said.

"And will you put some of them—with me—into your album?"

JoJo shrugged. "Sure."

"Okay," Winnie said.

They could hear Mom and Dad shouting downstairs.

"Let's go tell them the good news," JoJo said, taking her sister's hand. "And wish them a Merry Christmas."

Chapter 2

The Spear Bearer

JoJo's fourth-grade class was going to put on a play for the whole school.

"It will be about a princess who is really a peasant girl," said Ms. Waterford, their teacher, "and a peasant girl who is really a princess. We will need two girls to play the princesses and one to play the queen. Then we will need a bunch of peasants. We will also need a farmer, who has three sons, and some soldiers who guard the palace. There will be enough parts for everybody in the class. The peasants sing songs, so we should have people who like to sing. The soldiers carry spears. One of them has a speaking part. It's a very funny play."

JoJo and most of the girls in the class wanted to be one of the princesses or the queen. Most of the boys wanted to be the king or the farmer or one of the three sons.

When JoJo was not picked as either one of the princesses or the queen, she swallowed hard and looked down at the ground. As usual, Marie was picked for the queen, which was the best part. JoJo did not like to admit it, but she had been jealous of Marie ever since kindergarten. Everything Marie wore matched perfectly. And teachers always seemed to pick her for special things. When Ms. Waterford asked JoJo if she would like to be a peasant, she shook her head. "But the peasant girls wear pretty skirts and bright scarves on their heads. They sing really cute songs."

JoJo made a face. "I don't like to sing," she said.

"Well then," said Ms. Waterford, "you can be a guard. You can be the one who has a speaking part."

The class began to rehearse. The queen and one of the princesses wore pretty pink dresses and gold crowns on their heads. The king wore a purple robe and a gold crown. The peasant girls wore bright, flowered skirts and red scarves. The peasant boys wore red tunics over jeans and straw hats.

All of the guards had to wear black pants or leggings. They were given yellow and scarlet tunics, a helmet made of cardboard, and a long black wooden spear with a blunted point. JoJo played the guard who stood in front of the castle door. When the farmer and his sons came to the castle, demanding to see the king, JoJo was supposed to stop them by putting out her spear in front of them. "Wait here!" she told them. That was her speaking part.

Winnie said her class would be sitting right in front of the stage. This was the first school play she had ever seen.

"Don't expect much," JoJo told her. "It's a stupid play, and it's not funny."

"But you have a speaking part," Winnie said. "Don't you?"

"Two words," JoJo told her. "Marie's the one who has the biggest speaking part."

"She's so pretty," Winnie said.

JoJo made a face.

Winnie waved to JoJo from the audience. All of the classes were squashed together on the floor in front of the stage. JoJo had to stand very still in front of the castle door while the other guards marched around the stage. The play was a long one. JoJo could see from the faces of the children in the audience that they were bored. Nobody seemed to find it funny. Nobody laughed.

She was bored, too, standing there in front of the castle door, waiting to say her two words. The children in the audience began wiggling. The other teachers had patient smiles on their faces. Nobody was laughing.

The peasants kept singing silly songs about *hey nonny-nonny*, whatever that meant. They didn't sound very good. JoJo's arm was itchy, but she couldn't scratch it. She had to keep standing still, holding up her spear.

Finally the farmer and his sons arrived, demanding to see the king. JoJo lowered her spear in front of them. "Wait here!" she said. Then she turned. She was supposed to raise the spear against her shoulder. But she forgot. Instead, she held it out in front of her as she strode across the stage.

Unfortunately, the queen, Marie, came running out onto the stage at that moment. Very quickly. JoJo's spear caught her right in the middle of her pretty pink dress. Marie fell down. "Ouch!" she yelled. JoJo fell down on top of her, and the spear went flying across the stage. For the first time, the audience laughed. JoJo quickly got back on her feet and helped Marie up. Marie gave JoJo a shove and said some words that were not in the play. The audience went on laughing. It took JoJo a while to find her spear, which had fallen into a group of singing peasants. After she found it, she raised it up as she was supposed to do and marched off the stage.

The audience cheered and applauded. After the play, when all the actors had taken their bows, the audience stood and clapped. They kept applauding even after the actors had left the stage.

Marie was furious with JoJo.

"You ruined the play," she said, after it was over. "How could you have been so clumsy?"

But many kids in the audience did not t[...] JoJo had ruined the play. "You were the best," Winnie said. Other kids said the same thing. Some of them thought JoJo had knocked the queen down on purpose. Ms. Waterford looked angry at first. But when people kept telling her how funny the play was, she admitted that no audience had ever laughed so much as they had for this performance. She began thinking that maybe the next time she produced the play, she would have the guard knock down the queen on purpose—and maybe some other characters as well. She forgot to be angry at JoJo.

Some of the kids in her class kept teasing JoJo. But her friend Samantha and a few other girls were pleased. "Marie's always so cool," Samantha said. "But she sure didn't look cool rolling around on the ground when you knocked her over with your spear." Samantha lowered her voice. "Did you do it on purpose? Come on, JoJo, you can tell me."

"Of course not," JoJo insisted. "I would never do anything like that."

JoJo kept apologizing to Marie. But Marie stayed angry. She was sure JoJo had done it on purpose. JoJo knew she hadn't, but she began to think maybe the play wasn't so stupid after all. She wished she had a picture of Marie rolling around on the floor to put into her photo album.

Chapter 3

Swimming Lessons

When JoJo was six, Dad had taken her for
swimming lessons at the Y. By the time she was
nine, she could do the crawl, the backstroke,
the breaststroke, and the sidestroke. She could
also tread water for five minutes and swim back
and forth across the pool six times. She had
moved through the Pollywog group for begin-
ners to the Guppies, then to the Minnows, and
was now a member of the Silver Fish. Only one

group remained—The Flying Fish—where you learned to dive, and then you could join one of the Y teams.

When Winnie was six, Dad said it was time for her to take swimming lessons, too.

"No!" said Winnie.

"Why not?" Dad asked.

"You know why not," Winnie told him. "I hate swimming. I'm afraid of drowning. I never want to swim."

"Winnie," Dad said, "I know you were knocked down by a big wave when you were two. But that was four years ago. It's natural that you're afraid of the water. Swimming lessons will help you overcome your fear."

"No!" said Winnie.

Mom tried. "Maybe we'll buy you something special if you take lessons."

"Like what?" Winnie wanted to know.

"Well, maybe a new Beanie Baby."

"No!" said Winnie.

"How about two new Beanie Babies?"

Winnie hesitated. "Could I have the unicorn and the lion?"

"Yes, you can have both. Okay?"

"No!" said Winnie.

Then JoJo tried.

"Listen, stupid," JoJo said. "I'm going to tell everybody what a wimp you are."

Winnie shrugged.

"I'm going to tell Rosie and Jamie and Tommy and Alison."

"Who cares," Winnie said. "And besides, I already told them."

JoJo put her face up very close to Winnie's.

"If you don't take swimming lessons, I'm going to take back Fuzzy Bear. She was my bear first, and I just lent her to you."

"No, you did not!" Winnie shrieked. "You gave her to me because I was afraid of the dark. And you didn't want me to keep coming into your bed at night. If you take away Fuzzy Bear, I'll start coming into your bed again."

"Okay! Okay!" JoJo said. She pulled her face away from Winnie's. She thought for a while. Then she said, "If you take swimming lessons, I'll play with you every Monday afternoon from four to five. You can pick the game."

"Really?" Winnie grinned.

"Yes."

"Can we play school, and can I be the teacher?"

JoJo shuddered. "Okay—you can be the teacher."

"I'll take swimming lessons," Winnie finally promised. "But I want three Beanie Babies," she told Mom. "The unicorn, the lion, *and* the monkey."

While she was in the Pollywog group, Winnie clung to the side of the pool and howled if the instructor tried to pry her loose. But every Mon-

day afternoon, from four to five, she and JoJo
played school. And every Monday afternoon,
Winnie was the teacher, and JoJo was the
cranky student.

"You're a very good sister," Mom kept telling
JoJo.

After five weeks, Winnie was still a Pollywog.
The swimming instructor was now able to pry
Winnie off the side of the pool, but only if Winnie could keep her arms locked around her
neck.

By that time, Winnie no longer wanted to
play school on Mondays from four to five. Now
she wanted to play house. She was the mommy,
and JoJo was the baby.

"I don't know how long I can keep this up,"
JoJo complained to Mom.

After five more weeks in the Pollywogs, Winnie finally unhooked her arms from around the
instructor's neck. She let the instructor hold
her in the water, and she began kicking. Then

Winnie learned to float and rode around on a floating noodle in the shallow water with the other kids.

"This is fun," Winnie said. "And next Monday, let's play Cinderella. I'll be Cinderella, and you'll be the wicked stepsisters."

"Not anymore," JoJo said. "Enough is enough. From now on, you're on your own."

Winnie advanced to the Guppies. She learned to do the crawl, the backstroke, the breaststroke, and the sidestroke. She could also tread water for five minutes, swim back and forth across the pool a dozen times, and dive, keeping her head down and both legs straight. She moved quickly from the Pollywogs to the Guppies, the Minnows, the Silver Fish, and finally to the Flying Fish.

"She's the best swimmer in her class," said the instructor proudly, "and the youngest. She is just about ready to join a team. In a year or two, she will certainly be a star swimmer."

"And it's all because of you," Mom and Dad kept saying to JoJo. "You must be very proud."

But JoJo did not feel proud. Nobody ever said *she* would be a star swimmer. It was impossible for her to dive keeping both legs straight. She was not proud at all. In fact, she was sorry she had ever offered to play with Winnie on those humiliating Mondays. And it was hard finding out that there was something Winnie might actually do better.

But JoJo hoped that was the only thing. As soon as Winnie arrived in the Flying Fish, JoJo gave up swimming lessons and joined the Girl Scouts instead.

Chapter 4

Lice

Winnie brought home a note from Ms. Cranberry, her first-grade teacher. It said:

Dear Parents,
   I am sorry to tell you that a child in this class has head lice.

The letter went on to ask parents to check their own children's hair. It also explained what lice looked like, and how to get rid of them.

"Oh no!" Mom said as she inspected Winnie's head. There were no lice, but there were nits.

"What's nits?" Winnie wanted to know.

"Nits are the eggs that lice come out of," Mom explained. "They fasten onto your hair and make your head itch. They are very, very contagious. We will have to remove each one of them from your hair with a special comb and use a special shampoo to make sure they don't come back. We'll also have to wash all your sheets, blankets, and pillows. And your clothes and toys."

"Not my Fuzzy Bear," said Winnie.

"I'm afraid so," Mom insisted. "Unless you want to put her away in a plastic bag for a couple of months."

"No!" Winnie shouted. "I can't go to sleep at night without Fuzzy."

"Well then," Mom said, "I will have to put her into the washing machine. I'll be careful."

JoJo had stayed later at school that day for

a Girl Scout meeting. Samantha's mother dropped her off.

"Mom!" JoJo called as she came into the house. "Guess what? Our troop is going to sing at the Morrison Senior Center next Friday. Tomorrow, we'll start practicing at Samantha's house. How come there's a shower cap on Winnie's head? And why are you looking at me like that?"

There were even more nits in JoJo's hair than in Winnie's. There were also a couple of full-grown lice.

"I'll have to call Samantha's mother to warn her about the lice," Mom said grimly. "And you and Winnie will be staying home from school tomorrow."

"But I have to practice the songs we'll be singing," said JoJo.

"And what about my swimming lesson?" Winnie demanded.

"I'm very sorry," Mom said. "But neither of you can go anywhere until we get rid of the lice and the nits."

Later, when Dad came home, he checked Mom's hair. She had nits, too. Dad didn't have nits. Dad was balding.

"The three of us will have to stay in until we get rid of the nits and the lice," Mom said. "I won't be able to go to my book group tomorrow."

"That's too bad," Dad said. "But the three of you will be able to entertain one another."

"The four of us," Mom said. "You need to go shopping for us and do loads of laundry at the Laundromat. Our washing machine is too small to handle all the blankets and pillows."

Nobody was cheerful that day.

"Fuzzy's eyes are crossed," Winnie sobbed after Mom had lifted the loads of toys and clothes out of the washing machine. "And her fur is all in patches."

"I'm sorry, sweetie. I thought she was washable," Mom said. "But I promise you, as soon as we can, we'll buy you a new bear. A washable one."

"I don't want a new bear," Winnie cried. She cradled Fuzzy in her arms. "I just want Fuzzy."

"Fuzzy does look ugly," JoJo said. "But not as bad as my Leonardo Leopard. All his spots are faded, and most of his teeth have fallen out."

Dad brought home burritos for everybody that night. Usually, the girls liked burritos, but everything smelled like yucky lice shampoo. Even their favorite peanut-butter chocolate-chip-swirl ice cream smelled like it.

The next day was better. There were many phone calls. Both Samantha and her brother, Noah, also had nits. Rosie, from Winnie's class,

called. She had nits, too. So did seven other kids in the class. Even Ms. Cranberry had nits.

"It sounds like an epidemic," Mom said. By now, she was wearing a shower cap, too. "But at least nobody can blame it on us."

All day long, the phone kept ringing as more and more people reported in. Mr. Rice, the fifth-grade teacher, was out with nits, and so was Ms. Olive, the principal.

After the third shampoo, Mom couldn't find any more nits in either JoJo's or Winnie's hair.

"Thank goodness," she said. "I was afraid we were going to have to cut your hair very short if the nits didn't go away."

Between phone calls, the girls played hospital with Leonardo and Fuzzy. They made little shower caps for them out of plastic wrap and rubber bands. They fed them soup out of bottle tops. And JoJo operated on Leonardo's mouth. She even managed to sew some of his teeth back in. She also took timed photos of Mom, Winnie, and herself in shower caps.

The next day, there was no sign of nits or lice. But Mom worried. She thought there might be other kids at school who had lice. She was afraid JoJo and Winnie might become infected again. She was sure some of the rugs, dress-up clothes, and soft toys in many of the classrooms were still infected. The PTA agreed. They decided to send in a squad of mostly bald fathers and bald teachers over the weekend to help clean up each classroom. The squad carried all the rugs, dress-up clothes, and furry toys over to the Laundromat.

By this time, the girls did not have to shampoo their hair or wear shower caps. They were also getting used to Fuzzy and Leonardo, and some of their other strange-looking toys. The next day was warm and sunny. JoJo and Winnie went outside with Mom, and all of them rode their bikes around the neighborhood.

"I haven't gone biking in years," Mom said as

she wobbled down the driveway on her old bike.

She was a little rusty, but JoJo and Winnie were very patient with her.

Some of their friends, wearing shower caps, waved at them from behind their windows. Mom fell off her bike once and skinned her knee, and she also crashed into an unfriendly man. But they had a great time anyway.

Dad did not enjoy himself. He and the other people on the bald squad spent the whole weekend carrying laundry in and out of the school. By Monday morning, Dad's back hurt so much that he couldn't go to work. But JoJo and Winnie, with clean and shining hair, went back to their clean and shining school. The epidemic was over.

Chapter 5

The Tooth Fairy

"Julio Rosenkrantz says that the tooth fairy is really your own mother," Winnie said.

"Julio Rosenkrantz has a big mouth," JoJo answered. She was arranging her photos of a baby beluga whale into a bright blue scrapbook. It was for a school report.

"Julio also says Santa Claus is your mother, and so is the Easter bunny."

JoJo shifted two of the pictures around.

"Right!" she said. "Mom always runs around flapping her big ears and saying *Ho! Ho! Ho!*"

"He's not absolutely sure about this," Winnie continued, "but he says that God might be your mother, too."

JoJo put the pictures down and gave Winnie her annoyed look. "God is not your mother!" she told her. "You're six years old. You should know that by now."

"Well, I told Julio I didn't think so." Winnie watched as JoJo began arranging her pictures again. "Are YOU God?" she asked respectfully.

JoJo slammed her album shut. "No! I'm not God, and I'm not the tooth fairy, and I'm not Santa Claus or the Easter bunny. Do you understand?"

"Yes." Winnie smiled. "I'm glad."

"But," JoJo continued, "you might want to talk to Mom."

"Oh, I did," Winnie said. "And Dad, too."

"And what did they say?"

"Mom asked me what I thought, and I told her. I don't want her to be the tooth fairy. So she said I should just go on believing whatever I liked, and Dad said . . . I don't remember what Dad said. Anyway, Julio says they're not telling the truth."

"Well, forget about what Julio says. There are always kids who want to spoil things for other people."

Winnie came a little closer to JoJo and opened her hand. Inside lay a tooth. "It just fell out," she said.

"So what are you going to do with it?"

"Julio says I should put it under my pillow and pretend to fall asleep. He says I should stay up and wait. He says if I do, I'll see Mom come sneaking in. She'll take away my tooth and leave a dollar."

JoJo said carefully, "Isn't it most important that you get the dollar? Does it really matter who leaves it?"

"It matters to me," Winnie said. "I love the

tooth fairy. She has curly red hair and a bright green dress. And her wings sparkle with shiny sprinkles. They whir over my face when she comes."

"How do you know that?" JoJo asked.

"I just do," said Winnie.

Mom came down with the flu that afternoon, and she spent the rest of the day sleeping. That night, Winnie got into bed before her regular bedtime. "I'm so tired." She yawned loudly. She kissed Dad good night, and she kissed JoJo. Mom was still sleeping. "See," she told them. "I'm putting my tooth under my pillow. I hope the tooth fairy remembers where I live."

Dad shrugged and turned out her light.

"What are we going to do?" JoJo whispered to him outside Winnie's room.

"I'm not going to do anything," Dad said in a cranky voice. "Right now, I'm worried about your mother. She's got a high fever."

Winnie kept jumping out of bed that night.

First, she needed a snack. Then she was thirsty. Then she had to go to the bathroom. Then she needed another snack. Dad grew crankier and crankier. "Will you stop making all that racket, Winnie? Your mother is sick, and I don't want you to wake her up. Now go to sleep!"

The hours crept along. It was nearly eleven o'clock, and Winnie was still up. Dad had gone to sleep, but JoJo lay in her bed, wide-awake, listening. The house grew still except for Winnie running up and down the hall. "I must stay awake," JoJo said. "It's up to me to stay awake. I must stay awake. I must stay . . . I must . . ."

When JoJo woke up the next morning, she knew immediately that she had let Winnie down. But then Winnie came bursting into her ͻm.

ͻme! She came!" Winnie yelled. She

new dollar bill.

JoJo asked, sitting up in bed.

"The tooth fairy, of course. She came. I knew she would."

"Did you see her?"

"Well, not exactly, but I know it was her. I felt the whir of her wings on my face. Wait till I tell that Julio. He thinks he knows everything."

When Mom came staggering down to breakfast, Winnie told her about the tooth fairy.

Mom groaned. "Oh, no! I forgot. I was so sick yesterday—I must have slept through the whole night."

"I wonder what time the tooth fairy came," Winnie said. "I tried to stay awake but I couldn't."

"Neither could I," JoJo said, puzzled.

Dad was buttering a piece of toast. "I think she came around two-thirty in the morning," he said.

"How do you know that?" Mom asked. "You never wake up at night. You're the soundest sleeper of us all."

"Because she made such a racket," Dad said.

"But did you see her, Daddy?" Winnie wanted to know. "Doesn't she have curly red hair, a bright green dress, and sparkly wings?"

"I didn't see her," Daddy said, "but I sure heard her stamping around. I think she must wear hiking boots."

JoJo laughed out loud. She wasn't puzzled any longer about who had left the clean, new dollar bill. Mom bent over and kissed Dad right in the middle of his bald spot.

"Oh, Daddy," Winnie said patiently, "you just don't know anything about the tooth fairy."

Dad nodded and picked up his newspaper. "I guess not," he said.

Chapter 6

Take-Your-Daughter-to-Work Day

"Last year I took JoJo to work with me on Take-Your-Daughter-to-Work Day," Dad said to Winnie. "This year I'm willing to take you, if you want to come."

"Yes, I do," Winnie said. "I don't have to go to school if I go with you. And can we have lunch out?"

"Don't go," JoJo advised. "It was boring. All Daddy does is work on his computer or go to

46

meetings or complain to the other people in the office about the Head."

"What's the Head?" Winnie wanted to know.

"She's the big boss. Nobody likes her."

"Was the lunch good?"

"Oh, yes," JoJo said. "The lunch was great. It was in a big Italian restaurant, and Daddy said I could have anything I wanted. So I picked the lasagna, although the pepperoni pizza looked pretty good, too."

"I guess I'll have the lasagna, too," Winnie said.

"But everything else is boring," JoJo warned.

Dad worked in downtown Seattle, in a big office. He had a small desk next to other people who also had small desks. Everybody was very busy but friendly.

Dad introduced Winnie to a woman with short, red hair. "Winnie, this is Juliemays and her daughter, Caroline."

Dad and Juliemays took them both around

the office and showed them where the water-cooler and the rest rooms were. There was a big window on one side of the building with a view of Puget Sound.

"Naturally," Juliemays said, "only the Head has that entire view."

Caroline and Winnie talked about what they planned on ordering for lunch.

"Sometimes," Caroline confided, "I don't like lasagna. Sometimes I like pasta alfredo."

"The Head's calling another meeting at ten," Dad said. "It's supposed to be a short one, but you know her. She'll go on and on and end up yelling at me."

"What's pasta alfredo?" Winnie wanted to know.

"It's any kind of pasta you want," Caroline explained, "with a white cream sauce."

"Well, thank goodness I don't have to go," Juliemays said. "I guess she doesn't think I'm that important. But that's all right with me."

"Yuck!" Winnie said. "I hate white sauces."

"Well, would it be all right then," Dad asked, "if I left Winnie with you while I was at the meeting?"

"But sometimes I like ravioli," Caroline added.

The girls had a good time playing in Juliemays's office. She let them play on her computer when she wasn't using it. And she gave them lots of printer paper to draw pictures on.

After a while, Winnie needed to use the rest room.

"Well, you know where it is," Juliemays said. "It's down the hall and to the left. Right near the staircase. You go with her, Caroline, and both of you come right back."

Caroline and Winnie went to the rest room. Then Caroline wanted a drink at the water-cooler. They must have taken a wrong turn because they couldn't find it. Then they must have taken another wrong turn because suddenly they found themselves in front of an up escalator.

"Let's go back the other way," Caroline said.

"Let's go up the escalator," Winnie said. "Maybe we'll find a watercooler on the next floor."

Caroline shook her head. "I'm going back."

"Well, I'll just take a look upstairs, and then I'll come back."

"Okay," said Caroline.

Winnie went up to the next floor, and she did find a watercooler. She took a long, delicious drink and looked around her. There weren't many people sitting at small desks like on Dad's floor. Only a few, and the rest had their own offices.

She was about to look for the down escalator when she noticed that the up escalator went up another floor. When she arrived there, she saw that the escalator kept going up. There were

even fewer people there than on the floor be-
low, in bigger offices. Nobody noticed her.

It's like "Jack and the Beanstalk," Winnie
thought. She took the escalator up to the next
floor, where it ended.

She found herself in front of a big desk with a
bowl of flowers on it. But nobody was sitting
there. Behind the big desk was a partially open
office door. Winnie could hear music coming
from behind it. She walked around the big desk
and peeped through the door.

A woman was sitting inside, eating her lunch,
and listening to music.

"You'd better be careful," Winnie said. "If the
Head catches you listening to music, she won't
like it."

The woman sort of jumped in her seat and
frowned at Winnie, who was standing in the
doorway. Then she said, "Who are you?"

"I'm Winnie," Winnie told her. "My father
works downstairs."

"Oh!" said the woman. She was very pretty in spite of her frown, with blonde hair and lots of makeup on her face.

Winnie came into the room. "You'd better turn that radio off. The Head doesn't want people making a racket. What's that funny stuff you're eating?"

"How come you know so much about the Head?" the woman asked.

"Oh, my daddy talks about her a lot. So does Juliemays, and I guess everybody else who works downstairs. Your lunch smells funny. What is it?"

"Sushi," the woman answered. "But why are you wandering around by yourself?"

"My dad had to go to a meeting. He said that it was supposed to be a short one, but he guessed the Head would yell at him, and it would take longer. I was supposed to stay with Juliemays, but I got a little lost looking for the watercooler."

"Who *is* your father?" asked the pretty woman, tightening up her mouth.

"He's the one who runs the place down on the second floor. He sits next to Juliemays."

"Oh yes. Is that Peter . . ."

Winnie laughed out loud. "Nobody calls him Peter," she said. "Most people call him Pete. But sometimes Mom calls him Patootie Pie."

The woman smiled suddenly. She had pretty sparkling white teeth. "I know for sure it was a short meeting, and the Head did *not* yell at your father. In fact, she praised him very highly." She offered Winnie one of her sushi rolls.

"Oh, were you there, too?" Winnie asked. She picked a small roll, chewed it carefully, and said, "This isn't bad. What is it?"

"Smoked eel," said her new friend. "Here, try the calamari."

A very surprised woman suddenly came bursting into the office. "Oh, I'm so sorry, Ms. Brewster!

I thought Lorrie was at the desk. I took my break, and she said she would stay until I came back, but I guess . . ."

The woman just waved a hand at her. "It's okay, Melanie. I'll talk to YOU later. Just let Pa-tootie . . . I mean Pete, on the second floor, know that his daughter is up here with me. She'll be coming down in a little while."

"I really can't imagine how she got in here," Melanie said. "I can take her down right now."

"Later," said Ms. Brewster. "After we finish our lunch."

So Ms. Brewster and Winnie ate and chatted and laughed and listened to music and looked out her window at the beautiful view of Puget Sound. Later, Ms. Brewster took Winnie back downstairs.

"Your daughter is very charming, Pete," she said to Dad. "And *very* talkative."

Dad gave Winnie his unfriendly look when she said that. But then Ms. Brewster hung

around and talked to Dad and Juliemays, and all of them laughed and acted as if they were having a good time.

When Winnie and Dad finally got home, they told JoJo and Mom what had happened.

"I got worried when Winnie was lost," he said.

"You must have been even more worried when you found out where she was," said Mom, and they both laughed.

"I wasn't worried or bored at all," Winnie told JoJo. "I had fun, and I made friends with Ms. Brewster. She shared her lunch with me, and Daddy said I could have lasagna or pepperoni pizza and anything else I wanted. But I was too full from all the sushi, so I just ate a hot fudge sundae. Ms. Brewster said I could come back and visit her anytime, but Daddy said I'd better wait until next year. He said he needed at least that long to recover."

Chapter 7

Cool

"No!" JoJo said. "I don't want to go." She was looking down at an invitation in her hand.

"Who's it from?" Winnie asked.

JoJo handed her the invitation. "From Marie Bridges. Last week she said I was weird. I can't stand her."

Winnie opened her eyes wide over the invitation. "Wow!" she said. "Wow! Marie Bridges is inviting YOU to her birthday party. Wow!!"

"So?" JoJo said, hurt by the tone in Winnie's

57

voice. "So what if she is inviting me? What's so special about being invited to Marie Bridges's party?"

"Well, she's the coolest kid in the whole school," Winnie said. "Everybody copies her. Even the kids in *my* class. We all try to toss our hair the way she does. But I thought she hated you. Ever since that play when you knocked her over with your spear."

"She does," JoJo said. "But I hate her even more. She's always making fun of me. I know she's only inviting me because Mom and her mother have become such great buddies lately. It's all Mom's fault."

"But JoJo," Winnie said, "wouldn't it be fun going to her party? She hangs out with all the coolest kids in the school. Wouldn't it be great if you got to be one of them, too?"

"Not for me, it wouldn't," JoJo said. "Marie and her friends are boring. They all wear the same kind of designer clothes. They all listen to the same music and read the same books and

wear the same color nail polish. I'm not cool. I'm me. And I'm not going to that party. Period!"

But JoJo ended up going anyway. Maybe because Winnie kept acting like JoJo was suddenly the president of the United States since Marie had invited her. Maybe because the other kids in her class were also impressed. Even her friend Samantha was impressed. "Wow! You're going to a slumber party at Marie's house? She invited YOU! Wow!" Samantha said. And maybe, although she would never admit it out loud, JoJo had always secretly admired Marie.

JoJo panicked as soon as she arrived at the party. Marie was wearing a green Ralph Lauren polo shirt over tight black leggings. Her other friends were also wearing Ralph Lauren shirts except for Sarah, who had on a DKNY shirt, and Katie, who wore an Abercrombie & Fitch shirt. All of them were tottering around on high clunky sandals. They looked silently at JoJo's

pink floral shirt and matching pants from JC
Penney and then looked away.

Marie's parents took them out to dinner. They
went to a fancy restaurant, and everybody (except JoJo) said "cool!" when Marie's father told
them they could order anything they liked.

They kept saying "cool" all evening. Later,
when everybody (except JoJo) painted one another's fingernails a bright, iridescent green
color, they kept saying "cool." JoJo painted her
own fingernails a pretty pink color to match her
pink floral outfit, but nobody seemed to notice.
Finally each of the girls (except JoJo) pulled
on a long nightshirt that said JOE BOXER or
HERSHEY'S or COKE, and they all said "cool." But
nobody said anything when JoJo pulled on her
blue and green nightshirt from Sears.

Marie and her friends listened to music. They
took off their shoes and practiced some dance
steps. JoJo listened, too. She would have liked

to dance but felt shy and awkward. Why had she come? Nobody spoke to her. She sat by herself on the floor and wondered if she could say she had an upset stomach and needed to go home.

They talked about boys. "Mark is cool," Sarah said. The other girls giggled. "No, he's not," Marie said. "But Gabe is." "Yeah!" said the others. "Gabe is real cool."

Cool, JoJo thought. *I hate that word! Of all the words in the English language, I hate that word the most.*

The dancing grew a little wild. Katie started doing the chicken dance. She kicked out her legs and flapped her arms. One of her arms flapped out too far and knocked over a bowl with two goldfish in it. The bowl fell crashing to the floor. It broke, and water spilled all over. One of the fish landed inside a shoe, and the other flapped around desperately under a chair. The girls yelled and tried to protect

their bare feet from the broken pieces of glass.

JoJo was the only one who was wearing shoes. And the only one who thought about the fish. Quickly she jumped to her feet, picked both of them up, and then rushed into the bathroom. Gently, she dropped the two weak, dazed fish into the toilet bowl and watched as they suddenly came back to life.

One by one, each of the girls came and stood by her side. They squeezed into the bathroom and watched the two little goldfish as they swam comfortably inside their new bowl.

"Cool!" Marie said. She rested a warm arm on JoJo's shoulder. "Thanks," she said, smiling. "Now I owe you one."

JoJo shrugged, but she smiled back at Marie. For the first time that evening, she felt comfortable and happy. She even took pictures of the goldfish and all the girls grouped around the toilet bowl. Each of them wanted a copy. "Cool!" they kept saying, but JoJo didn't mind. Maybe "cool" wasn't such a terrible word after all.

Chapter 8

The One in the Middle

Winnie did not like being the baby in her family.

"You get all the attention," she complained to JoJo. "Just because you're older."

"But you get away with more," JoJo said. "Everyone expects more from me because I'm the oldest."

"And you have the bigger room," Winnie grumbled, "and the pretty afghan Grandma made for you when you were born."

"She made you one, too."

"I like yours better."

"You like all of my stuff better than yours. I'm supposed to be jealous of you, not the other way around," JoJo pointed out.

"I hate being the youngest," Winnie said. "Nothing is worse than being the youngest in a family."

JoJo didn't argue because she liked being the oldest. But sometimes when she saw Winnie snuggling up in Dad's lap, or Mom kissing Winnie two or three times when she only kissed JoJo once, she almost wished she was the youngest.

About a month before Christmas, JoJo noticed that a lot of whispering was going on between Mom and Dad.

"I wonder why they keep whispering to each other," she said to Winnie.

"Maybe they're going to buy us something special for Christmas," Winnie suggested.

"Maybe," JoJo said grimly. "They always stop talking whenever we come into the room."

"You're right," Winnie said.

"But yesterday," JoJo continued, "I heard Mom talking to Marie's mother on the phone. She was saying something about our house being small but . . ."

"But what?" Winnie wanted to know.

"She stopped when she saw me. And she had that kind of guilty look on her face. I wonder . . . no . . . it couldn't be."

"What couldn't be?" Winnie wanted to know.

"Well, I think they're too old . . . but maybe Mom is pregnant. Maybe they're going to have a baby."

"No!" Winnie shouted. "*I'm* the baby. I don't want a new baby!"

"I thought you didn't like being the baby," JoJo reminded her. "If they had a baby, you wouldn't have to be the baby anymore. You'd be the one in the middle."

"I don't want to be the one in the middle," Winnie said, tears rolling down her face. "You wouldn't have to change places if there was a new baby. Just me."

"I had to change places when you were born," JoJo told her.

Even though it was a long time ago, JoJo remembered. She remembered what a new baby meant. It wasn't so bad at first. A tiny baby nestled in a blanket and grown-ups made silly goo-goo noises. But the baby didn't stay tiny for long. JoJo reached over and patted Winnie's arm. No, the baby would grow bigger and bigger. First she would sit in a high chair and spit her food all over the place. Then she would crawl into their rooms and mess up everything. She would make a pest of herself, as all babies did. Winnie was sniffing at her side. JoJo felt an unfamiliar swell of tenderness toward poor Winnie. She rested an arm on Winnie's shoulder.

Poor Winnie! She had no idea what she was in store for.

The girls decided to confront Mom and Dad.

"What's up?" JoJo demanded.

"What do you mean?" Dad said.

JoJo did not like the phony innocent look on his face. She did not like the way Mom turned toward him and grinned slyly.

"We want to know why you keep whispering to each other. We want to know what's happening," Winnie cried.

"Well," said Daddy. "If you must know—"

"Yes?" JoJo interrupted.

"It's a surprise," Mom said. "And you're going to have to wait until Christmas to find out."

"I hate surprises!" Winnie shouted.

"I don't think you'll hate this one," Dad said.

And they didn't. It had floppy brown ears, a white body with big brown spots, and a tail that

kept wagging and wagging whenever either
Winnie or JoJo picked him up.

"We had to wait until he was weaned from
his mother," Dad explained, "before we could
bring him home. But why did you say you hated
surprises, Winnie?"

"Because we thought—"

"Never mind," JoJo interrupted. Even though
they were safe now, she did not want to give
Mom and Dad any ideas. "What do you think
we should call him, Winnie?"

Winnie did not hestitate for a minute.
"Baby," she said. "Because now he's the baby in
the family, and I'm the one in the middle."

"And I'm still the oldest," said JoJo. "So
everything's exactly as it should be. Right,
Winnie?"

"Right," Winnie agreed.